For Holly, the most perfect person

About This Book

The illustrations for this book were created digitally. This book was edited by Deirdre Jones and designed by Carolyn Bull. The production was supervised by Bernadette Flinn, and the production editor was Jake Regier. The text was set in Papercuts, and the display type is Skizzors.

Little, Brown and Company
Hachette Book Group
1290 Avenue of the Americas, New York, NY 10104
Visit us at LBYR.com

First Edition: February 2024

Little, Brown and Company is a division of Hachette Book Group, Inc.
The Little, Brown name and logo are trademarks of Hachette Book Group, Inc.

The publisher is not responsible for websites (or their content) that are not owned by the publisher.

Little, Brown and Company books may be purchased in bulk for business, educational, or promotional use. For information, please contact your local bookseller or the Hachette Book Group Special Markets Department at special.markets@hbgusa.com.

Library of Congress Cataloging-in-Publication Data
Names: Cutler, Marcus, 1978– author, illustrator.
Title: I do not eat children / by Marcus Cutler.
Description: First edition. | New York, NY : Little, Brown and Company, 2024. | Audience: Ages 4–8. | Summary: "A monster claims he would never eat a child as the children playing around him suspiciously disappear one by one." —Provided by publisher.
Identifiers: LCCN 2022052545 | ISBN 9780316474726
Subjects: CYAC: Monsters—Fiction. | LCGFT: Picture books.
Classification: LCC PZ7.1.C935 Iad 2024 | DDC [E]—dc23
LC record available at https://lccn.loc.gov/2022052545

ISBN 978-0-316-47472-6

Printed in China

APS

10 9 8 7 6 5 4 3 2 1

I Do Not Eat Children

Marcus Cutler

L B
Little, Brown and Company
New York   Boston

I do *not* eat children.

I would *never* eat a child.

What do you think I am . . .

. . . a monster?

Wait, are you suggesting that I *do* eat children?

Well, maybe it is *you* who eats children.

Not me. I *love* children.

BURRRRRRRRRRRRRRRRRRRRRR—

—RRRRRRRRRRRRRRP!

Oh, pardon me.

Now, what was I saying? Oh yes . . .

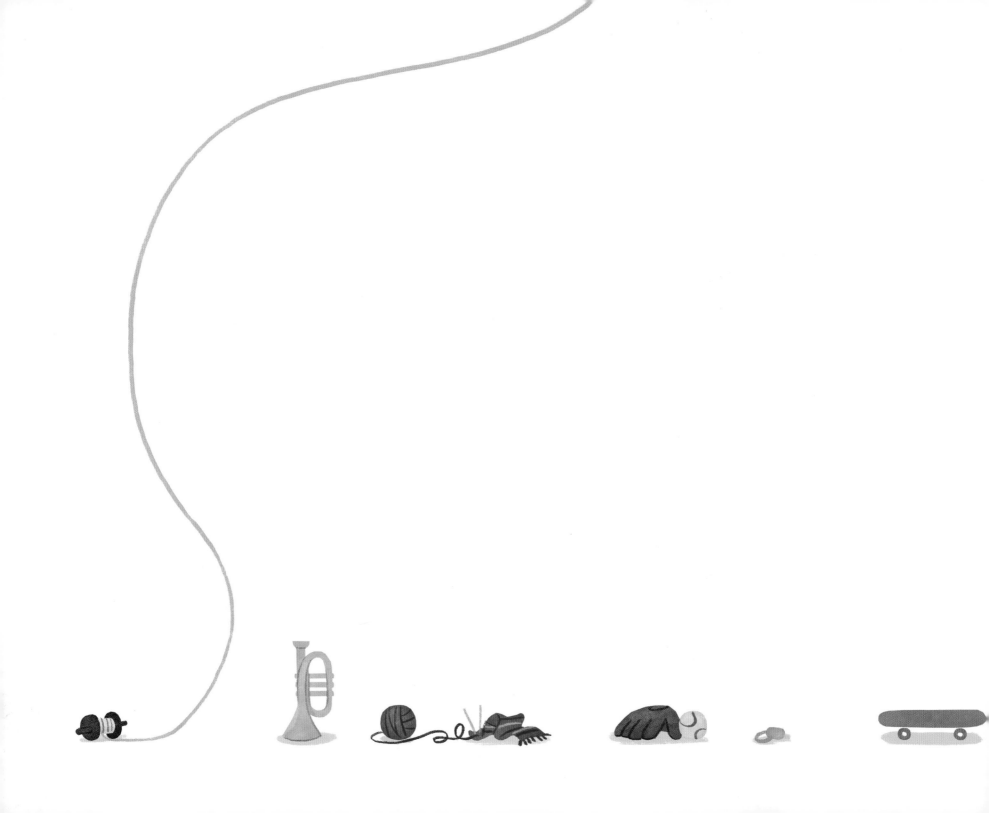

I do *not* eat children.

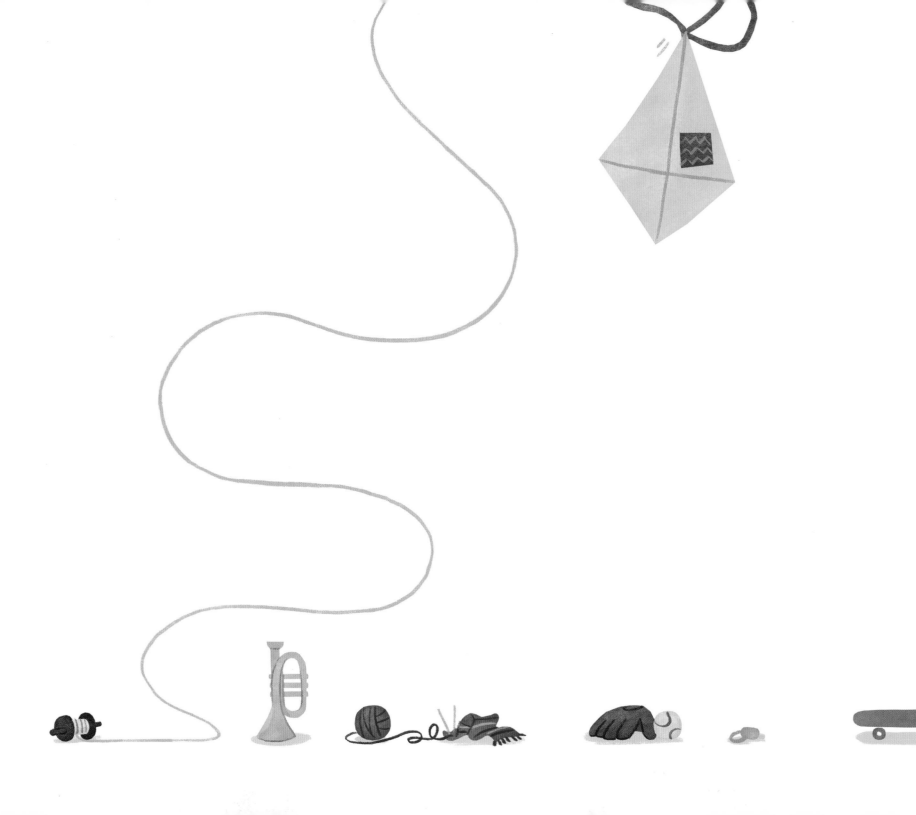

I *do* eat liars.